WILLWALKER
Adventure

WILL WALKER

Adventure

A. ALEX COME'

ARPress
ILLUMINATING IDEAS.
EMPOWERING VOICES

ARPress
45 Dan Road Suite 5
Canton MA 02021

Hotline: 1(888) 821-0229
Fax: 1(508) 545-7580

Ordering Information:

Quantity sales. Special discounts are available on quantity purchases by corporations, associations, and others. For details, contact the publisher at the address above.

Printed in the United States of America.

ISBN-13:   Softcover   979-8-89330-054-3
                eBook   979-8-89330-055-0

Library of Congress Control Number: 2024900838

"Dedicated to ELIZABETH my loving daughter, who has been waiting on this short story for some time."

Contents

It was chilly that fall evening. The cold northern wind blew at every shutter creating an eerie sensation in the body and minds of all those still awake. Sleep seemed to be a thing of fear, a thing of forgotten necessity.

The story I'm about to tell, however, was no part a dream and in no way an everyday thing. This night, there was something I was not aware of; something soon to happen, something horrible, something that would embed itself into my memory forever.

My name is Will Walker and I'm not a cop or a reporter, just an ordinary guy with everyday dreams and ambitions. The story I'm about to tell, however, was in no part my imagination and certainly not an everyday thing.

It all began on the night of October 20th. My fiancée Kimberly Holland and I were driving home from a late-night movie. I had decided to park a while and, well, strike up a conversation with Kim; one I was thinking might turn into an agreeable 'heated' discussion.

That particular evening, we pulled of the main highway onto an abandoned dirt-road called Slayer Lane; an old Farmhouse drive well overgrown with large dangling tree branches and weed patches that reached the car windows. The lane ended at an old, abandoned farmhouse disquieting enough to have unnerved the true grit right out of the late great, John Wayne.

Once we were parked, the car lights were out, and I had my strongest arm and fastest hand around Kimberly, she wasted no time starting the conversation, "Will, I don't like it here. Let's leave!

Well, I have to say, if you're an all-American red-blooded guy… actually…if you're an all-Russian, Italian, Irish, French, Dutch or any other nationality red-blooded guy, then you can appreciate the gravity of hearing those disheartening words. So, being the gentleman I am, I did the perpetual red-blooded male thing...I begged!

"Oh, come on Kim! You are letting that silly female imagination run away with you. What have you got to be afraid of, after all, I'm here." She made a face while grabbing my trained hand. "First, bad choice of words, *silly female*. Now let me reiterate, NO! I have got the creeps. I mean it, I want out of here."

For as long as I live, I'll never forget it, with a sour face I reached for the ignition and that's when the sound pierced through the black darkness around us; the most chilling, bloodcurdling scream ever; and to make things worse, it started a chain reaction, because simultaneously Kim screamed too, right in my ear!

All that TV stuff about heroes running to the rescue immediately filled my head but emptied back out again even faster. With what had to be the shakiest hand in the State of Indiana, I started the car and tore out of there like a scared Bat escaping from the Devil's Dinner Table; I just knew whatever had caused the scream was now chasing after us with the sole purpose of murder on its mind.

It took us ten minutes to reach town, another five for Sheriff Davidson to calm us down and a good five more to explain just what happened. Finally, with the Sheriff and Deputy Lou Micheles in the front seat, and Kim and I huddled in the back, we left town speeding for the old farmhouse. With red lights whirling and the siren wailing, road signs and telephone poles flew past the Squad Car in blurs. If you have ever ridden the Aerosmith Roller-coaster Ride in the Magic Kingdom and it didn't satisfy you, catch a ride with Lou Micheles.

When he applied the brakes...finally, and turned onto Slayer Lane, two things flashed in my mind: first, I gave personal thanks to the Creator for getting us here alive, and second; be it jitters, intuitive thinking, or plain old gut feeling...call it whatever, but something inside my head flashed like a big giant, mega warning; tell Lou to turn the car around and get out of here, get away before it was too late. At least wait for daylight. But it did not happen.

Squeezing Kim's hand, I glanced out through the window. I could not remember ever seeing a night so dark and freaky.

"Over there Lou, those Pines, that's where we were parked." Kim pointed a finger and Lou pulled to the spot. The House sat all by itself. In what used to be a front yard, there towered four dead trees grotesquely silhouetted against the chilly night sky. And all around them and covering what use to be a well-manicured lawn grew an ocean of high weeds and briers dancing in the wind.

The place looked ancient, forbidding. Shutters hung askew at the windows; the old roof had large patches of missing shingles with black jagged holes where sheets of plywood had rotted and fallen through. Pieces of broken glass sat menacing in every broken window; like obscure dark eyes staring at us. I could almost feel them following my every movement. Swallowing hard, I expected a horde of The Living Dead to come staggering out forming a big circle around the car; bare bones and dangling skinned hands banging at the windows, rotted smelly bodies wanting in; just one bite, just one single bite and.

No warning...Lou activated the powerful patrol car's spotlight. Scanning the house and immediate area around it, he made three slow, careful sweeps. When he shut it down, Sheriff Davidson turned to Kim and me. "You two stay in this car and DO NOT GET OUT OF IT. Understand?"

We both nodded and he added. "Keep the doors locked. Here take this." He handed us a flashlight; we both took hold of it at the same time, struggling for it, I won!

Davidson continued, "Use the flashlight to keep an eye on the area around the car. If you see anything at all, you yell and yell loud. And just in case we're far enough away and don't hear, honk the horn and flash the lights. We'll come running." Kim assured him she would, and I assured him rather she did or not, I certainly would! He ignored me, and handed me the car keys. "Take these, climb here into the front seat and stay there!"

Then he and Deputy Micheles left, quickly swallowed up by the darkness. Kim and I locked the doors as ordered. Thinking about that horde of The Walking Dead again, I, being the gentleman I am, suggested Kim sit extra close to me just to be safe.

The moonlight covered everything with dull, hazy gray light. We sat for hours, waiting. Well maybe not hours, but a long time. Long enough that we both agreed at least one of them should have returned to the car by now. Fifteen more minutes passed, and still a no show.

Finally I told Kim. "Something's wrong, I feel it! Maybe we should rev up and charge into town for help?" Kim made a face. "WHAT? Are you kidding?"

"Yeah, I told her weakly. "We'll wait one hour then go look for them". Kim said it again". WHAT?

This time I rebutted with compromise, "Okay, thirty minutes and we go take a look".

"No" she said. "We'll go in five minutes".

"Ten". I rebutted a second time.

Her face twisted, solidified. I felt as if I were sitting in the car with one of the Walking Dead ready to pounce on me and eat my face.

It was time to defend myself. "Sweetheart, you do realize there's safety in being safe".

Kim snarled! At least I think that was what it was. She held up her hand, showing five fingers for reinforcement, "Count them!" She ordered.

I gave a nod while staring at her hand; thankful bone and skin were all intact and my face wasn't missing a chunk.

"Okay, five it is." I told her, deciding to not remind her I was the man, and she should be listening to me! Sometimes I am just too nice.

It was the fastest five minutes of my life. Unlocking the door, I pushed it open; listening as it squeaked loud into the stillness of the night...stillness of the night! The words sounded like the title of a Vampire movie. The very thought of the creatures, even possibly being real, added willies to my willies. Half out of the car, one foot on the ground, I hesitated; thinking what if they. Kim pushed me out. The look I gave her was not one that said thank you.

In the night sky there were only a handful of Stars with a cold distant Moon glaring down at us. I paused starring up at him. I could see the dark-silvery eyes, nose, and mouth; he looked sad, and I knew why; he was heartsick over the fact we were probably about to be murdered! Kim gave me another little push for motivation.

Our flashlight dimly lit the path to the front door of the house. It stood open; wide open, like the starve-craved mouth of a starving behemoth monster waiting for that first bite of young human flesh.

The limited beam was not exactly overwhelming and it created a strong overtone of apprehension. Standing motionless at the doorway looking in, the sight was enough to discourage a platoon of Combat Ready Marines from wanting to enter.

Long clusters of Spider webs were everywhere; silky sticky strands hanging like streamer-traps all over the ceilings and fixtures, waiting to capture innocent victims. I detested the creepy, eight-legged predators. To Kim, not a worry, she would let them craw up her arm and sing to them as they moved. To me, the gross little fiends were no more than big eyed, silk-stringing pet's-of-the-Devil.

Lowering the light to the floor added still another dimension to the fear-factor; a herd of fat over-sized Rats were scurrying everywhere across the floor in all directions. One thought popped into my head; what was it the rodents had been eating to have blown them up to such an enormous size? They were in fact FAT! FAT! FAT!

This was it, I made up my mind this was far too risky a place to take the girl I so dearly loved. We were not going in; that's when Kim gave me another motivational push.

I stumbled through the doorway and into the house. That push accomplished three things: I was now inside the house, nothing had killed us getting here, and Kim heard me use a word she had probably never heard before.

Standing quiet and near motionless, I chewed on my lip thinking. When we had first arrived, the spotlight from the car had shown the front door closed, now it was open. That meant Davidson or Micheles or both had to be in here somewhere. But why had neither returned to the car. WHY, WHY, WHY!

Squeezing the flashlight tight in my hand and Kim right behind me, another thought came flashing through my mind. In the back seat of the Patrol Car Kim and I had wrestled for possession of the flashlight! I believed I had won. But truth be known, she had outsmarted me... she let me win!

CHAPTER 2

The wind pushed and howled through the open door and shattered windows. It was a challenge just to not turn and run. And in addition to my borderline case of Arachnophobia, was a new addition of fear; the countless number of Plump Beer Bellied Rats scurrying non-stop over our feet and between our legs. Their relentless scampering just wouldn't stop.

Kim and I stood frozen. What to do? My strong personal instinct was to turn and charge right out the door we had just come through. Then Kim came up with her solution… "Will we have to find them. Do something!"

Instinctively my male manly survival mode flashed in my head. If these numberless game players wanted to play; we'd play…FOOTBALL! It would be 'Walker Stud Man vs the Fat Rat Scampers'. I decided to punt. One after another I booted the fatty thin-tailed competitors across the room and through the darkness, gaining two points for every thump. The goalpost landings sent warning squeals to the others; get out, run, go find a haven.

I enjoy a good Football game; and this was educational. Kim and I learned the little brained Rodents must communicate, because soon all but a few, left the field. Feeling relief, we continued with the search, moving deeper into the dark interior. In my mind, there was no shaking it, I kept remembering the scream that had started it all.

Our eyes were adjusting to the shine of the flashlight. We now stood in a large room, a parlor by the looks. Remains of old furniture lay strewn about: a couch rotted and mildewed, several chairs turned upside down, end tables covered in dust and spider webs, and a fireplace on the far wall with a large corner hutch lying face down on the hearth.

Scattered papers covered the floor. Carefully making our way through the sea of paraphernalia, we moved into a hallway.

It was here, I became aware that something was biting, or burrowing into my arm. It was stinging! Dear Lord, all I could thing off was a poisonous Black Widow. Frantically I swung the flashlight with every intention of killing it dead. The light came down hard and Kim yelled; "Ouch", what the hell are you doing? You smashed my fingers." Her tone was not friendly,

Following a bad word under my breath I whispered, "Sorry, I thought you were a Black Widow!". The look I saw glaring through the flashlight beam did not show a happy face.

"You mean," she told me, "The Spider that kills her mate once she's bread?"

Following a short rubbing of her fingers, Kim once again shared her house-of-fright continuation; she pushed me onward again; this time a bit more motivational.

Moving forward, I glanced over my shoulder and whispered; "You know, if we get married, I don't think I want to have children."

We moved on into another room; this one housing ceiling to floor shelving. With dozens of its outdated books still intact, we drew the conclusion that at one time it had been a very well-kept Den and Library. All four of the walls stood covered with shelves, except for the distant north wall opposite the doorway. Here, the selves had been built around a large picture window, its glass divided into little square sectors, all broken out leaving odd, shaped fragments. Through them, blew the harsh cry of wind pouring in with eerie tones of whining and whistling.

It was spooky, and I wanted so much to turn and get out of this house, but Kim was insistent the two of us, armed only with a flashlight; search and find two highly trained, well-armed and experienced Police Officers searching the premises; both believing we were safely locked away in the Patrol Car.

I had to wonder, did Kim consider that our being here, unannounced, doing what we were told not to do, might very well accidentally get us shot and killed by either one of these fine, wonderful professional Law Officers.

Turning to leave the room, we were about to the doorway, ready to exit, when the wind suddenly stopped as if someone had turned off a switch. The room fell silent as a mortuary. No sound, nothing moved, not even us. Kim's sharp painted nails had returned to sting and bite me again. I nixed using the flashlight this time, but intensely suggested she lighten up!

We both stood motionless, ears straining, waiting for the sound to return. I wondered where Sheriff Davidson was and cursed myself for not waiting for him inside the car. I should have insisted. Then, as suddenly as it had stopped the wind returned. We were reborn; our legs filled once again with strength, our hearts began to beat, and we wasted no time getting out of that room.

Once again in the hallway, although reluctantly on my part, we continued, this time without the need of a push-motivation. The hallway ended and infront of us stood a door, and to our left the landing of a great stairway going up. We opened the door and looked. It led down into the basement. A decision needed to be made. If we continued, it would be go up or go down.

I presented Kim with my choice, "We need to get back to the car." And this time I said it in a voice firm with Will Walker man-authority!

Kim, I will say, does from time to time disagrees with my quick and decisive man-authority. But to my surprise, she agreed, "Okay."

I smiled with relief, then she added, "But first, we search the basement."

This time I put the light beam to my chin and added the man-authority look..."Kim, there is no freaking way we're going down there!"

She pulled the flashlight to her chin. "Will, you are the man and I respect that. However, I am the one you love and would die for if necessary. So put the man-authority attitude aside and understand...as soon as we have searched the basement for those missing Officers, we will indeed return to the car. I promise."

Shaking my head, I said it softly out loud. "Mars and Venus"! As I turned to the Basement Stairway, I thought to myself...the stupid, senseless, and foolish things we do for Venus".

With just the small flashlight guiding the way, our decent took quite some time. Halfway down, Kim mentioned hearing an odd noise. I tried to ignore her; my imagination alone was bad enough.

When we reached the bottom step, we stopped. It turned out Kim's imagination was reality. There was for certain a strange noise...and not just one. She had heard a hundred and more. She heard Rats!

Using the light's beam, I scanned the basement floor. The Nasty Fat Rodents looked to be wall to wall. Opposite and to the right of the stairway, an unusually large congregation was not doing much moving about; just an occasional circular movement or deadly nip at one another. They were huddled on top of something...and Dear God, I thought; don't let it be what I'm thinking.

Turning the light on Kim, it shined in her eyes, and she pushed it away. I asked if she had something I could throw. She looked at me like it was a dumb question. "I don't have anything," she said, "I do not have my purse with me it's in the car. Throw your wallet, it rarely has anything in it anyway."

"No way", I told her, "It's got a picture of you in it. She melted, "That's so sweet".

Shining the light around us, I found a few miscellaneous items hanging from spikes on the wall beside the stairs. Grabbing an old metal horse brush, I spoke more to myself than Kim, "This will work fine." With a shaky hand I pointed the beam of my light to the rat-infested hump, I threw it hard for effect. I missed. I couldn't see it but I knew Kim rolled her eyes.

Whispering a word, I don't frequently say, I searched the wall again and found an old muskrat trap hanging by a short chain. "Let's try this one more time". I said. The rusted chain jingled as I pulled back and threw, it landed too far to the left. "Damn"! This time I yelled that word aloud.

Pulling the light from my hand Kim sighed with agitation. "What are you doing," I snapped. "I'm a football fan", "not baseball pitcher!" She ignored me. Searching the wall, she found something of her own to throw. I could not tell you what it was. She aimed the light, drew back, then let the object fly. It hit right on target, landing just below the head of the mound. A decent size portion of the rats scattered and for only a few seconds, time long enough, we saw just what I had hoped it would not be. Kim screamed for the second time that night in my ear.

It was only a matter of seconds before the fat rats returned to their feasting table, but we had seen enough. It was a girl, a woman.. She was naked, her mouth still open as if she had died screaming. Not all her face was there. Kim vomited. And I fought the urge myself.

Pulling ourselves together we turned hustling back up the stairs. By this time, Sheriff Davidson who had heard Kim scream, was bolting his way through the house, gun drawn. He was calling for us and we met him at the top of the stairs.

"Are you kids alright? When we did not answer he repeated himself a bit more sternly. "Are you two okay"? "We gave him a nod.

"What was that scream all about"?

I figured I better answer. "There's s a woman down there, or at least a part of a woman".

"What the hell do you mean a part of a woman?"

"Sheriff, there are hundreds of rats down there eating her". All Davidson could say was, "For crying out loud". He moved past us and descended the stairs.

Approximately forty seconds went by, and we heard his gun go off. It fired six times. Six times Kim jumped. Sheriff Davidson was angered and disgusted in what he had seen.

The gunfire brought Lou Micheles running this time. He asked what had happened, so I filled him in. Sheriff Davidson returned to the top of the stairs, gun still in his hand. Immediately he began barking orders.

"Will, take Kim to the car, and stay there this time. Lou, you go with them, get on the radio and call the city. Tell them to send homicide and an ambulance ASAP. Tell them we need an exterminator just as quick. And while you are at it, give the state boys a call.

Turning to leave I heard him tell Lou he was going to finish checking the rest of the house. On the way to the car two thoughts popped into my head: one; would Sheriff Davidson reload before resuming the search, and two; what else, or who else, would he find.

CHAPTER 3

Back at the cruiser Lou notified everyone he was suppose too. When finished he repeated the same thing Davidson had told us earlier, only with slight modification. Lock these damn doors and STAY HERE this time. Climbing out, he disappeared into the night.

Laying my head back on the seat I closed my eyes. Getting the sight of that girl out of my head was no easy task. Hands down, rats had jumped up to first place on my list of things I hate the most; Eyes closed, I prioritized the list of dislikes: Rats, Spiders, Cockroaches and Kent Briars; Kim's old boyfriend!

I did not know who the woman was down there in that basement, but whoever she was, she died a horrible death. Someone had put her there knowing the rats existed. What a cold blooded S.O.B. Question is, was he still around? The possibility made me glad we were back in the car with the doors locked.

I woke up! I must have fallen asleep. It could have been seconds or hours, I didn't know, but Kim was screaming, and I was instantly awake. Startled, I sat up straight and looked at her. She was holding a hand over her mouth pointing toward the front of the car. Turning I looked. "Holy Crap!" It must have stood over seven feet tall. Whatever it was, it was coming straight for the car. In less than ten strides it had reached the front bumper peering eerily through the windshield at us. I felt like the proverbial Goldfish. We had to do something, and I was the man for the job...at the top of my lungs I screamed for Sheriff Davidson. The next thing we knew that seven foot whatever, was lifting the front of the car like a sesame-street toy. Kim and I slammed against the back of the seat. The vehicle was in an almost vertical position, resting on the back bumper. That is when we heard the two shots ring out. Immediately the thing let out with one heck of a loud bellow and gave the car a jolting thrust. We flipped completely over crashing onto the roof.

The last thing I remembered was hearing the light bar shatter and the creaking of medal. I was not sure, but I thought another shot sliced through the night; then blackness came, and I slipped into the world of unconsciousness.

When I awoke, I was not sure what to think. There were colored lights swirling with Police and Firefighters all over the place. I was now laying on the ground and Sheriff Davidson was kneeling beside me. Grabbing his arm, I asked about Kim. When he smiled and assured me she was fine, relief washed over me in a joyous flood.

Looking around at everyone, I felt a heck of a lot safer. Except for a little buzzing in my head, I felt pretty good. Sheriff Davidson helped me to my feet and made sure I was able to stand. When I flashed him a quick smile and nod of assurance, he let go of my arm and I left to join Kim.

She was leaning against a State Police Car, arms folded and staring at the ground.

"High Babe." Looking up she broke into tears. "Oh Will, thank God". She threw her arms around me, and we hugged one another tight, but only for a second. Our private moment did not last long.

"Is your name, Will Walker"?

I turned to see a man in his mid-thirties dressed in a light-colored trench coat and wearing a Fedora Hat. "I'm Captain Plucousky, homicide. I'd like to ask you a few questions".

Standing there, amid all the headlight beams crisscrossing and red and blue swirling lights swirling, he took on the appearance of a hologram. I also thought two more things, although they were weird; first, I could not believe just how much this man resembled Maxwell Smart, Agent 86, and two; I was feeling famous, like the main star of a B rated cops and robbers movie. Silly thoughts I know, but we've all had them, right? RIGHT...?

I puffed my cheeks and told Plucousky, "ask away, Agent 89. He did not get it or had been worn out from hearing it a lot. He corrected me, "It is Captain Plucousky.

Without further a due he went on. "You and the young lady were in the patrol car when this guy, or whatever, flipped it over, right"? I nodded and he continued. "I realize it was a trying experience and happened quickly, but could you give a description of this guy"?

I found describing him no problem, "It was at least seven feet tall with hands the size of buckets. Had overly broad shoulders and it never stopped showing its teeth, and drooling. And those teeth, incidentally, were extremely disfigured. It had dark hair that hung down to its shoulders and wearing what looked like a white colored robe. The ears were big, human looking, but large, and the nose was wide, almost pug-nosed. But the oddest thing of all were the eyes. I mean, I realize it was dark and all, but those eyes were yellow, almost glowing. It all sounds crazy I know, but that's what I saw".

Kim nodded in agreement then added. "And one more thing, Captain, and this is strange, but if I had to say there were human likenesses, it would be the fact it looked Afro-American. And as you can see, being Afro-American myself, I'd recognize that fact pretty quickly". Plucousky glanced over at me, probably because I was white. Then glanced back to Kim. "You're sure"? She nodded and Plucousky looked back to me then.

"What about you, Mr. Walker, did he look black"? Afro-American, I corrected him. "Yes, Kim's right, he did, but my primary focus had been those eyes and teeth". Plucousky asked a few more questions then closed the pad he had been writing on and stuck his pen into his pocket. "Okay, he said with a warm smile, "I appreciate your time". He turned and walked off, disappearing amid the sea of people.

Still leaned against the car, I took Kim's hand and held it. "You know...," Suddenly we were blinded by bright flashes of light. The press had found us.

There bombardment of questions hit us the same instant we began seeing little black dots. Each time we'd get our pupils straightened out, they'd take more pictures; we were answering questions one after another and it seemed as though they'd never end.

Reporters must take Interrogation 101 in college, because eventually they had us saying things that we weren't even sure happened. It all grew so chaotic. Finally, feeling like a hounded Johnny Depp on a Saturday night in downtown L.A., I grabbed Kim's hand and broke through the crowd of these Paparazzi impersonators.

They followed with their cameras still flashing and tongues wagging! My list of things I hate the most changed again: it was now Paparazzi, Rats, Spiders, Cockroaches and Kent Briars. And since I'm not Johnny

Depp; although some have said, I say modestly, that I do resemble him, I put two and two together; the Paparazzi probably thought I was Johnny here to just gather experience for an upcoming movie character. That would explain my feeling of being a movie star in a B-rated cops and bad guy's flick! Right?

Regardless, the News People remained relentless. But just as my last twine of patience broke, Captain Plucousky came along and saved us. He ordered the people-vultures to go feed on somebody else and we slipped away to a darker, quieter spot. Plucousky turned out a not so bad guy. "They're almost as bad as the rodents in the basement, aren't they"? He said.

"Worse." Kim replied.

I followed her comment with a question. "Captain Plucousky, why do you think that thing, attacked the car?

He hesitated. "Truth"?

"Yeah, please" I nodded.

"I believe it may have been after you and Ms. Holland" I looked at Kim then back. "Why"?

"My guess, it figured you two had seen it and feared you might be able to identify it. It was more than likely the one that had thrown the woman into the basement. I would say that, about the time you raced out of here that first time, it was just about up to your car, but luckily your timing was right, and you got away. More than likely, it figured you would return with the authorities and so it waited, believing the risk of being caught outweighed the chance of murdering the two people who could identify it. Just be thankful Deputy Micheles was a good shot. He did not kill it, but his shots scared it and that saved your lives".

Plucousky stopped talking then and stuck his hands in his pockets.

I glanced at Kim. "Well, I'll be. We owe Lou a steak dinner".

"I'm afraid that won't happen". The captain added.

Kim and I looked at him. "NO" I said, "Why? He s okay, isn't he"?

Plucousky shrugged. "I'm afraid not, he's dead". My heart sank and Kim's eyes filled with wetness.

"What happened"?

"After he shot the thing, it ran for the woods. Against Sheriff Davidson's orders, he ran after it. By the time the Sheriff got out of the house and into the woods behind him, it was too late. The thing had overpowered Micheles. The Sheriff found his body lying beneath a pine tree. The thing had mutilated him". Captain Plucousky cleared his throat. "You know, I should not be telling you all this, but I have my reasons. I think this thing may try and get at you again. So, for the time being, I want you to stay in town and go out at night as little as possible".

The thought of being restricted upset me a little, but when I thought of the possible consequence, I found myself willing to go along with it. Suddenly I yawned. Kim saw me and did the same. We were both ready for a good night's sleep. Plucousky saw us and got the message.

"You two look worn out. I will arrange transportation to take you home". He could not have guessed how thankful we were. In no time we were in a patrol car speeding toward town and home. My mind was going over everything that had happened. As soon as we reached the outskirts of town, I told the policeman to drop us off at Sheriff Davidson's office so I could pick up my car, then I'd take Kim home and he could return to the crime scene.

Sitting quietly in the back seat watching the colorful city streetlights streak in and out of the car, I wondered to myself: Does this thing have the intelligence, or instinct, whichever ability it possessed, to track Kim and I to our homes? If it did…God help us.

CHAPTER 4

Next morning, I was up at seven. I scrambled four eggs, popped up two toast, poured a sixteen ounce glass of orange juice then sat down to eat while waiting for the morning paper. One toast down and halfway through the eggs it banged against the front door. Excitedly I went after it.

Back at the table I slipped the rubber band off and opened it up. Sure enough, there we were, and with a four-column article. They must have been up all night throwing this one together. According to the story, it was either an invasion from another planet or our tranquil small town had become the Transylvania of North America.

Smiling, I set the paper aside and took a bite of eggs. Naturally with my mouth full the phone rang. It was Kim and it was good to hear her voice. "Will, did you read the paper"?

It was not good morning, hello my love, I'm glad you were not murdered during the night by the yellow-eyed monster. Did you read the paper?"

Washing the eggs down with a sip of orange juice I told her, "yes, in fact I did". Not letting me finish, she began a ten-minute homily on the evils of the freedom of the press. But it worked out well; I was able to finish breakfast while throwing in a: yes, yep, sure, and a couple dozen you bet babe, between bites.

Since it was Sunday, Kim wanted to visit her grandmother right after church service.

Grandmother June was one of those rich old ladies who told it like it is and paid little attention to what people thought. Of course, she had the money to nourish such a personality; and she could, from time to time, get under my skin, yet I thought the world of her. With certainty she'd have something to say about last night.

Kim finally wore out her vocal cords and hung up. I headed for the shower. During the final rinse it dawned I hadn't locked the front door last night. I didn't get mad at myself though, since when you think about it, it wouldn't have mattered; a locked door would never have kept that thing out if it wanted in.

Kim and I pulled into her Greatgrandmothers around 12:30. Mammaw June we should call her, met us at the front door, which she rarely did, usually that was done by the butler; this time, however, she handled it personally, wearing one of those expression's that say, you're freaking in for it.

Silently we followed her hunched figure into the parlor where she had the butler bring in coffee. No sooner had he poured us a cup when she started in. "I see by the paper you two had a little excitement last night." She was looking right at me. "Let me tell you something Will Walker, if I weren't old and feeble, I'd spank your sorry ass. What were you thinking, taking my sweet great granddaughter to such a place, and so late at night?

My wit being as quick as my trained hand, I retaliated respectfully. "Well, Mammaw June, we had heard the house was haunted and naturally, us being young and full of adventure, and since we happened to be in that area, we thought...

Mammaw cut in not batting an eye. "Don't try and con my Mississippi born ebony ass; you thought no such thing; you were hoping to get into Kimberly's panties". I blushed. "There see" she said pointing an old, wrinkled finger, if you were Afro-American, like Kimberly and me, I'd have never caught you in that lie. Blushing is like a lie-detector test to you white folks".

Too embarrassed to defend myself, Mammaw continued. "Hell, I was young once myself. We did our share of bumping in the night and in the daylight too sometimes", a small, faint smile showed at the corner of her lips, but disappeared quickly, "you young folk today, you all seem to think parking and doing it is all there is to life", she pointed her finger again, "well let me tell you something Will Walker, you could learn a lot from the old days, from us old fogies, if you'd take a notion to listen".

Mammaw June paused long enough to take a sip of coffee. She closed her eyes savoring the flavor, then set her cup down and looked at us, seriously. "Let me tell you all a true story. That place you were at last night, it's more than haunted, its evil. Kim and I looked at one another then slid to the edge of our seat.

"Evil"? I asked, "Evil how"?

Mammaw June leaned back in her chair and took in a deep breath. "Twas an awfully long time ago, during the Civil War, some of the folks in this area were pretty active in the Underground Railroad, the secret movement of runaway slaves from the south into the Northern States and Canada. That house you were at served as a Station, a hideaway. One night in 1863, the family there was hiding a group of runaways, most folks say seven or eight, some say ten or twelve. How many really isn't important".

Mammaw June paused to pick up her coffee cup and leaned back again. "On one night, July 4th it was, a gang of slave hunters, demon bastards I call them, rode up to that house. They searched, found the runaways, then herded everyone outside, including the white farm family. The biggest and strongest male Black person was singled out of the group. His hands were tied behind his back, and he was beaten beyond recognition-then placed on a horses back to be hung. But; before that rope took his life, they forced the poor soul to watch through his swollen eyes as the farmer, his wife and three children were butchered by sword and axe, and their bodies thrown into the basement where legend has it, rats; hundreds of them, scurried in from every direction, pouring out of the bushes, woods, across open fields; each and every one racing for the basement; to feed on the bodies of that poor family".

Mammaw June took a sip of coffee and made a face; the coffee was cold. Picking up the carafe the butler had left for us, I refilled her cup. Thanking me with a nod she continued. "According to legend, from that day on the rats remained, and for some strange reason, were impossible to be rid of". She stared into the contents of her cup a moment, than continued on, "Anyway, as the rope was place around the unfortunate Negro's neck, he pronounced a curse, vowing to return from the grave and for so long as that house should stand, he would kill any and all white-skinned people who so much as set foot upon the property. The slave-hunters laughed; he was hung, and so the legend began".

I started to speak but Mammaw raised a hand. "There's more. That night, as it turned out, there had been a witness; a highly respected and prominent citizen named J.W. Peters. He ran to the nearest Army Post and reported just what he had seen. Every available soldier was dispatched to track down the murderers. Sadly, they were never caught. I watched as Mammaw sighed thoughtfully. "For the next ten years, the old legend held true and anyone who for any reason, dared approach the old house was found dead the next day, their bodies torn to pieces. Fear of the house grew stronger as time passed; until one day, two decades later, the mysterious murders stopped. The rats remained, but over the years grew less and less in number, until one day there were almost none. What you saw in that basement last night, was the way it looked that night in 1863. The curse had returned"!

Mammaw June fell silent. Her story had left the hair standing on the back of my neck. I had a thousand questions for her and didn't know where to begin. Gulping down my coffee, I made a face, mine had grown cold too; but I hardly noticed. About the time I opened my mouth for the first question the butler walked in. "Excuse me, Mrs. McBeth, you have a telephone call; Hawaii I believe".

She smiled briefly. "Thank you, Howard. I've been expecting it. I'll take it in the study". Howard helped her to her feet, and she turned to us. "I suspect I will be on the phone for some time, feel free to help yourselves to the coffee. If you'd like something to eat, Howard will get it for you. Make yourselves at home".

We thanked her but turned down her offer, rising to leave. We were halfway out of the room when she called out after us. Stopping, we turned.

"Will", she said, "you stay away from that house. Do you hear"? Smiling, I told her not to worry and we left.

It was now pushing 1:30. My stomach was begging me to feed it, so I asked Kim if she was hungry. She said yes so, we wheeled into an A&W root beer stand. I was so wrapped up in my thoughts, I hardly noticed the long-legged redheaded waitress with the short-shorts and low buttoned red silk blouse showing far-to-much cleavage. Marching to my side of the car she asked, "What's your pleasure"? Why couldn't she had simply said, may I take your order?

When finished writing it down, she cocked her head and smiled long and wide. Turning then, she walked away, and I mean, walked away. And that'smile, it had been so flirtatious; but then I am a realist; she was obviously a Johnny Depp groupie and, well, hey, if you look like someone, you look like someone. I couldn't default her for thinking me to be a movie star.

Following her with my eyes I wondered what it was about a woman that...suddenly Kim was shaking me. "Hey, lover boy, stuff your tongue back in your mouth you are getting the floorboard wet. Typical male", she said shaking her head, "a smile, a little cleavage, and it's hey kitty, kitty; come play with the pole".

Again, being the realist I am, I understood things were not going so well. It was time for a little Will Walker charm. "Hey", I told her, eyebrows wrinkled with shock, "you know me better than that. You won't believe this, but all the while I was watching her, I was thinking about you; how lucky I was to call Kimberly Holland my fiancée. I swear if you were that girl, we'd never get along. I mean, you saw her, she is a tease, a flirt, a showoff; unlike her, you don't have to show off what you've got, what you have shines through naturally, like a beautiful sunset. You are the perfect girl for me, and I love you just the way you are, and who you are". I paused, taking her hand. "And I'm going to step out here and just say; if there was anything about you at all that I could change, it would be one thing and one thing only; that you be exiled to the Garden of Eden, with me, and we spend the rest of our lives there, alone and forever, for all eternity".

Kim stared into my eyes, as if studying me, and I knew just what she was thinking; God, I'm going to jump right into this man s arms and plant a bunch of little tender kisses all over him. However, that wasn't quite the way it went. "Will", she told me still not smiling, "you may not be a box office draw movie star, a New York Times best-selling author, or highly paid quarter back for the Indianapolis Colts, but you do have something in common with all of them; you're definitely a pro".

I started to express my surprise when Red came around the corner carrying our tray. Quickly I covered my face with both hands. I heard her hook the tray over the window edge and ask with puzzled expression, "Would you like anything else"? Not looking up I shook my head. "No, that's all, thanks".

When she was gone, I uncovered my eyes and looked at Kim. "See", I expressed warmly, "it's truly only you that I have eyes for". A wisp of a smile showed at the corners of Kimberly's mouth. "My love", I told her, "I understand you being upset, even a little jealous, that's okay; it's a human characteristic. In fact, if you think it might make you feel a little better, even though you don't have too, if you want to unbutton a couple of buttons and show a little cleavage for me, well; I just want you to know I'm here for you".

CHAPTER 5

Following the episode at A&W, I dropped Kim off at work; she's an athletic trainer and aerobics Instructor at the Health Club downtown. Normally I'd have joined her at the club and worked out, since it was my shift off from the Firehouse, but I skipped it this time and drove instead to the library.

Locating a spot near the door I parked and hurried inside. I was not after a book. I began a search for one of the three Librarians that worked there. Two were checking books in and out, so I walked the main floor glancing down isles. In one of those isles, I found Librarian number three, Lyle Garson. Lyle was the library manager; part-time. In his full-time he was a dairy farmer. An older man, mid-sixties; he was highly respected and recognized by the literary locals as more a historian than librarian. He knew me and when I approached, he smiled, speaking first.

"Will. How are you"?

 "Fine, Lyle".

We shook hands. "Can I help you find something"?

"Actually no", I told him quietly. "But if you've got a minute I'd like to talk with you.

Lyle nodded. "Sure".

I followed him through four isles, around a corner and into his small office. He walked around his desk and extended his hand toward a chair sitting beside it. "Have a seat."

"Thanks." I told him.

"Now, what can I help you with"? He paused, grinned, and added. "If I were to guess, I'd say it is about that house you were at last night with Kimberly. How is she by the way?

"She's fine." I smiled. "And actually, it is about the house. You read the morning paper"?

"Yes, in fact I did. Heck of a story.

"That is for sure, Lyle. Look, I was wondering if you knew something about the Legend of that old place; especially information about the man who had witnessed everything the night of the murders, J.W. Peters".

Lyle leaned back in his chair. "Well, let us see. J.W. Peters was just about the richest man around in those days, dabbled in real-estate, hotels, and thoroughbred racehorses. He lived on a local farm which back in his day looked more like a ranch; maybe you know the place, its s now called Garson Farms."

Surprise showed on my face. "You mean your place, your dairy farm"?

Lyle smiled. "Yep, that's the place. It was their Peters lived and died.

"Wow", I said with surprise, "and doesn't your property border that of the old farmhouse? Lyle nodded but I didn't give him a chance to talk. "So, what do you know about the Legend"?

It didn't take Lyle long, he told me word for word the same things Mammaw June had said, emphasizing grandma's warning. "Will, I don't know if you believe in ghosts, or demons and such, but let me tell you. There is something terrible about that place, something evil and not of this world. Stay away from there. Stay far away".

When we finished talking, I rose from the chair, ready to leave, then hesitated. "Lyle, I have one more question. I had heard tell Garson Farms has been in your family for three hundred years. How is that if J.W. Peters owned it during the Civil War, you own it now? Are you in some way related to J. W. Peters"?

Lyle grinned, pausing. It wasn't a warm grin; more like one to stifle a sudden prick of feeling uncomfortable. Following several long moments of staring at me in silence, he rose from his chair. "Will, I really must get back to work. It has been nice talking to you, tell Kimberly I said hello".

He walked to the door and opened it for me. Looking at him I apologized. "Lyle, I'm sorry if I offended you. I didn't mean to get personal".

He nodded curtly. "That's alright. Good day, Will". As I ambered back to the car, the wheels in my head were turning. I may have been a little out of line about the generation thing, but Lyle certainly didn't have to be so abrupt. There was something he was not telling me, something he was hiding. And if so, what?

Pulling onto the street I drove back to the spa and picked up Kim. It was her day off too; she had gone in to teach an aerobics class for a friend on vacation. So, when I arrived she was waiting for me.

Still dressed in workout clothes: black spandex, white Nikes and tee-shirt tied mid-drift; I watched her walk to the car where I waited. She was so incredibly beautiful; like a model sauntering down the runway: slight precious sway to the shoulders, breasts afloat, and her eyes big, alive, and stunning. I was a lucky man, and I'll admit, there was a little truth to what Mammaw June had said, I would have enjoyed...well, to put it in a friendlier motion... a Hot Decision that night!

When she got into the car I asked if there was anyplace special, she needed to go or wanted to do. When she said, "Yeah, let's go to my place."

I smiled, put the car in gear and pulled away. "Whatever you're beautiful beating heart desires, my love." I told her. I did not get a smile back. She just looked at me shaking her head. I made a face.

"What"?

I held her hand all the way there, but my thoughts had shifted to the old farmhouse; pondering over the things that had happened there, and on the things, thank God, which could have happened there, but didn't. So wrapped up in my thoughts was I, Kim had warned me twice to slow down, but I did not hear her. She of course would have called it...did not t listen. Either way, there was no third warning, out of nowhere, red and blue lights showed up suddenly, flashing in my rear-view mirror.

Not letting Kim see the embarrassment on my face I pulled over. I took out my wallet and grabbed the registration; it didn't take long for the officer to get from his car to mine.

"May I see..."

I handed them out the open window before he finished the old proverbial. I smiled for him. He would just warn me!

"You were doing fifty in a thirty-five." He said. And on his face was one of those expressions that screamed his thoughts; 'do you think you are some spoiled high school boy jerk, breaking the law thinking it'll impress your lady"?

Honestly, I didn't care for his mental opinion, but, if a warning was all I got then I was more than happy to put up with it. However, the end result was just as the French are so fond of saying; Que sera sera – what will be, will be. Dolefully, I watched him write out the ticket then hand it to me. I didn't bother smiling again when he put it in my hand.

I drove away. Kim patted my knee. "Don t worry sweetheart", she said ever so tenderly, "I love you, and promise not to be an, I told you so".

I had to defend myself. "Kim, I never heard you, I really was lost in thought."

She smiled.

Before I knew it we were pulling to a stop in her driveway. After getting out of the car I put an arm around her and walked slowly to the house. Once inside, she poured us a glass of wine and we settled relaxingly on the sofa. What I had on my mind wasn't on hers.

"Will", she asked, "who do you suppose owns that old farmhouse now"?

My thoughts were not parallel to hers. But I liked the subject. "I don't know Kim", I answered, "but now that you mention it, that's a heck of a good question". While I thought about it, she excused herself and went into the bathroom to shower and change. I got up from the sofa and grabbed the telephone; Mammaw June would have that answer. It was getting late and fortunately she was still up. When I popped the question, she gave me a name and rural address. Quickly I told her how beautiful she was, then hung up before she started in on the importance of us staying away from the old place.

Gulping down my wine I yelled excitedly for Kim but she didn't answer. I yelled again, louder; again, there came no reply. My brow furrowed with concern. Setting my wine glass down on the coffee table I hurried toward the bathroom door. Gently laying my ear against it I could hear the shower running. I tapped on the door, "Kim. Are you all right"? When she didn't answer this time, I turned the knob and pushed the door open with a forceful shove, practically falling on the floor.

Recovering, I glanced to the shower. My heart stopped! Kim was there all right, leaning against the shower edge, arms folded. The curtain was pulled back out of the way. She was smiling and naked. The thought that popped into my head was, for lack of a better way of expressing it...dirty. It was apparent I needed a shower too!

CHAPTER 6

Having showered I hustled Kim to the car. By the way, its s amazing how a hot-steamy shower can put a smile on your face.

As I opened the car door for her Kim asked where we were going. My answer was simple. To visit Mr. Donald Trensdale Wright the third, who resides at 2460 Myester Drive. Kim frowned. Who's he and where is that"? I knew she'd ask. I explained about the call to her Mammaw as we got underway. Neither of us really knew exactly where Myester Drive was located. Mammaw had told me it was about fifteen miles out of town heading west; so, I just pointed the car and drove. We stopped twice so Kim could ask directions and thanks to my divergent insistence she do so, we found it quickly.

It turned out Donald Trensdale Wright the third, was a farmer. Pulling up the long drive to his house I noted dozens of different pieces of farming equipment, some rusted beyond use and others new. The place looked like the world's largest farm implement wrecking yard.

When I brought the car to a stop Wright stepped out of his big farmhouse and onto the porch to greet us. He was clad in a blue and white checkered wool shirt, bib coveralls, black rubber boots, ball cap and double-barreled shotgun. I whispered to Kim, Green Acers we are here!

She looked at me funny. What?

Not taking my eyes off the man with the shotgun I told her never mind. Rolling down my window I forced a smile, "I believe you are Mr. Wright?"

The moment I said it I frowned. Who would have ever guessed Will Walker would be saying that to another man!

Donald with the shotgun spit a chew of tobacco and spoke from the porch. What do you young people want?

As briefly and concise as possible, I explained the chain of events that had happened from the time we left the movie that night, up until our pulling into his driveway. All the while I had been talking, he seemed extremely interested and I saw that as a good sign. I wrapped up the story and waited for an invitation to come in and sit a spell. After staring a moment, in cold dead seriousness, he replied. I'm going to tell you just one time. Get your asses off my land. If you ever come back, I will shoot the both of you. Now get of my property.

I didn't try to reason with him. Turning the car around, we pulled out of the drive and headed back toward town. Once out of sight Kim asked if I thought he really meant it. I told her I didn't know, and that was the extent of our conversation until we were back at her place. Once there I poured us a glass of wine and relaxed on the sofa. The wheels in my head were turning again.

Deep in thought, I sipped three glasses while Kim cooked supper. When it was ready, my favorite, spaghetti, and meat balls, we sat down to eat. Halfway through it I told her. As soon as it's dark we're going visiting again.

Who this time? She asked.

We're going to pay Donald, the shotgun farmer another visit, only a covert drop in this time.

Kim has always been levelheaded and trusting in my decision making. "Are you freaking nuts"?

Shrugging, I told her matter of fact. "I thought you might take that approach. So, it's okay if you stay here where it is safe. I can go alone. Girls are expected to be frightened and too afraid to do things like this".

Kim pointed with her fork, smiling; but it wasn't friendly. "Where you go, I go. And not because you psyched me into it, or I have to prove something, I'm going because you are a daft little boy in, yes, a beautiful big boy body, who should be eating Ridlin like candy, and who without me to look after him; would get his sorry gluteus maximus shot off".

I could not help but smile. "See, you really do love me."

Looking down at her plate she stabbed a piece of meatball saying, "Shut it and eat your spaghetti while we are both still alive. Who knows what may happen tonight!"

We waited three hours before leaving. By the time we got there it was so dark we had to hang on to one another to keep from getting separated. We parked the car a half mile away and cut across a field. A dim glow of light from the house was all we had to guide us. It was taking forever so we picked up the pace and began a slow steady run; the light began growing closer. I couldn't get rid of the image of Wright holding that shotgun; yet I was enjoying the excitement of all this too.

The light from the house was glowing brighter and brighter, my heartbeat was quickening, then I ran smack into the barbed wire fence. I barely had time to bounce back before Kim, trailing right behind, slammed me into it again. It was all I could do to keep from yelling aloud. It tore the front of my shirt, and I could feel warm blood trickle slowly down my abdomen. I didn't tell Kim about that, only that it had ruined my shirt. We climbed over the fence and continued, at a slower pace.

Eventually we reached the farm-equipment lining the drive. Hiding behind it we worked our way up to the corner of the house, then quietly to the first window; the one that had been acting as our guiding light. Carefully I peeked in. Wright's home looked like an untidy antique store. On every wall hung several types of old-fashioned clocks. The entire room sat clustered with colonial furniture. I knew very little about antiques, but I did spot two dining chairs I would have sworn to be original Chippendale; there were old guns, vases, paintings, China and almost everything else imaginable. I drew the conclusion Donald Trensdale Wright the third, was very well off for an old country farmer.

The dark night around us was so quiet we could hear the ticking of the clocks inside; the sound was eerie, like something out of a horror movie. Temporarily satisfied, we both sat on the ground beneath the window. I took the opportunity to check my wounds. They had stopped bleeding. Kim started to whisper something when we heard the phone ring inside the house. It was so loud it sounded as though we were sitting right next to it. I stood up and looked in again. Wright was coming straight toward our window. I ducked with my heart caught in my throat. The phone must have been on a table right under the windowsill. We heard him pick it up and listened to a one-sided conversation.

"Wright here. Today? How? Serves him right, the old fool. Yeah, they were here too. I told them I'd shoot them if they came back. The young punk didn't even try to argue, ran like a rabbit. There was a slight pause then Wright exclaimed. "TONIGHT! I was just getting ready for bed. Yes, for crying out loud I'll be there!"

The conversation ended and we listened as he cradled the phone. I figured it was time to make the great escape. When Wright left the widow, we left the farm, happy we didn't buy it.

Back at the car Kim asked. "I wonder who he was talking to, Will"? "Yeah, I wonder too". I told her. "I also wonder what they were talking about. Let's follow him". Kim said with excitement.

I couldn't see her but I looked at her. "Now who's freaking nuts"? The thick blackness prevented me from seeing it, but my beautiful Kimberly smiled. I guess you are rubbing off on me, she whispered. She reached out to stroke my hair, but missed, poking my eye with her finger. I yelped at the pain and the silence of the night made it sound as if we were in the Swiss Alps. When the pain subsided, I made Kim kiss it, and I felt better.

We waited there in the car with forced patience. There were a few stars in the sky and the moon was but half a man. A shiver ran through me, and I turned up the collar of my shirt, wondering if my cuts were making me a little shocky. Out over the fields fireflies were glowing and in the tall grass along the country road, crickets chirped noisily. I shivered again and explained to Kim the grave dangers of shock caused by the loss of body heat; I suggested she slide across the seat and share the warmth of her body.

Unfortunately, the headlights of Wright's truck came on the same instant Kim began to move toward me and snuggle…she froze to look on. I had one thought, freaking farmers! The engine started and we both watched as Wright idled down the drive and out onto the road. The man drove like a racetrack maniac. It was near impossible tailing him.

Following a sixteen-minute ride at eighty mile per hour, he finally slowed and made a left turn onto a dirty drive. We drove past to throw off any suspicion. Quickly turning around, we watched as his taillights disappeared. There was no need in following any longer. We knew where he would end up; by an old rundown farmhouse filled with rats.

CHAPTER 7

I put my foot in the fan and held it there until we reached town. My cell phone was dead, and Kim had forgotten hers. While focused on the road I explained she needed to start concentrating on what she was doing instead of thinking about making hanky-panky all the time. She must have been concentrating, she didn't reply.

Just south of town I came to a screeching slide at the only payphone in town. Dropping in fifty cents I dialed, then listened as the phone rang six times before someone answered.

"City Police Department, Sergeant Love".

"Hello sergeant, is Captain Plucousky on tonight"?

"One moment please". The phone went to elevator music. I looked at Kim and frowned, while rolling my eyes. I always thought of Elevator music as music made for Dead People.

Then he was back. "No sir, he s off duty and will be back at eight tomorrow. May I give you his voice mail or take a message"?

"No". I told him. "Can I have his number? This is an emergency."

"One moment." The phone went to elevator music again. I was ready to climb the phone both. Seconds passed as fast as a Turtle knowingly moving to a worm covered fishhook so he could be caught and made into Turtle Soup."

"What is your name."

"Will Walker". I told him.

"He paused a second. "Yes, okay, I have a note hear saying I may give it out to you. Do you have a pen"?

"Don't need one, go ahead."

"The number is 449-7707".

I repeated the number so Kim could hear it. After thanking him I hung up and dropped another fifty cents into the slot. I dialed and the phone rang and rang. I was really on edge now. Pretty soon I would be the one needing that Elevator Music. Sweat ran into my eyes and I found myself fighting to keep from shouting colorful metaphors. Slamming the phone down I dropped in another two quarters. If I had to call one more number, it would be straight to my lawyer, to file bankruptcy.

"City Police Department, Sergeant Love."

"This is Will Walker again. I'd like to leave a message for Captain Plucousky after all."

"With me or voice mail, sir"?

"Through you." Tell him Will Walker called, to please return my call ASAP. Tell him I think there has been another murder. Tell him if I'm not home I'll be out at the old house. This is extremely important Sergeant Love. If you can track him down, I would appreciate it. Thanks."

I hung up hoping the line about another murder would put a crab in his pants and get him dancing. Between Kim and me we had enough change for just one more call. We dumped it in, and I dialed the Sheriff's office. Astounded, I listened as the receiver was picked-up on the second ring.

"Sheriff's Office, Deputy Johnston."

"Yes, is Sheriff Davidson in"?

"No sir. I'm afraid he's out on patrol. May I be of assistance"?

With a raised, notable frustrated voice, I explained who we were and the situation. The deputy responded the way a good law enforcement officer should. He asked where we were and told us to wait right there. So, I hung up and we did just that – but with a little pacing. Within six minutes Deputy Johnston himself came pulling up in his patrol car. His window rolled down and he asked. "Are you Will and Kim"?

"Yes, we are". I told him quickly.

"Leave your car here and get in."

We climbed into the back seat and closed the door. Johnston turned, looking through the heavy wire barrier. I tried to reach the Sheriff on the radio, but he must be off the air.

"I'll have to go myself so just point the way".

It seemed like hours before the deputy pulled the car to the shoulder of the highway opposite Slayer Road. He got out, closed his door quietly and spoke to us in a soft voice. "Okay. You two stay in the car. If I am not back in thirty minutes, drive the car into town and wait at the Sheriff's Office until he arrives".

Not wanting to agree, I did anyway; then watched as Deputy Johnston moved up the drive toward the old house. We watched until he vanished into the blackness.

This waiting was more frustrating than the telephone calls. I couldn't sit still. We should have gone with him. My ears strained to hear something. I didn't know what; perhaps a gunshot, or my name being called, even a scream or something, anything!

I didn't crack it much, but I lowered the widow a little for better sound. The crickets were gone and there were no fireflies lighting the fields any longer. Out of its darkness the night had given birth to a wind that now swayed the trees, rubbing their branches together like chimes, leaves rustled and a faint howling whistled through the cracked window. A storm was coming.

I sat as long as I could, turning I told Kim. "This is it. I'm going up to the house". Her logic came to the forefront again. "Are you freaking nuts?

"I have to", I told her, "you stay here in the car and lock the doors. If I or the deputy are not back in fifteen minutes, take the car into town like planned". Kissing her cheek, I got out and closed the door quietly. Turning, I started up the drive crouched and running. In the front yard I kneeled behind the first Weeping Willow tree and studied the house. It was dark, no light, and no sign of Wright's truck. Moving from Willow Tree to Willow Tree I made my way into the small section of Pine and around back. It was there I found the truck. Leaving the security of the Pines I dashed over to it and looked inside; empty.

While moving around to the front I tripped over something and cursed quietly into the darkness. I glanced down, that something was Deputy Johnston. He was lying face down on the ground, so I kneeled and rolled him over onto his back. Reaching out I felt for a pulse, but my fingers slipped into something wet and warm; it was his throat, it had been cut. I made a face and shuttered.

The knees of my trousers were growing wet, so I rose quickly to my feet. I looked at the illumanized hands on my watch. Eight minutes remained before Kim slipped behind the wheel and raced away to town. Fear, and the instinct to survive pounded in my brain. There was no doubt the thing had murdered Deputy Johnston and was still out for more blood; mine! I had to get back to the car and go for help with Kim. I knew I could never outrun this killer-thing, so I hoped I could at least outthink it.

Slowly, carefully, I began moving again, back-tracking to the car. There was nothing I could do here except get myself murdered; and I did not like that idea at all. My pace was slow in the darkness. I checked my watch periodically knowing that eventually I'd have no choice, I would be forced to go onto the road and make a run for Kim and the car. I hated the very thought of it, but as they say, time was of the essence. Or, as I felt deep, deep inside, time was Life or Death!

Not daring to use the road for as long as possible, I found myself clumsily tripping and walking into low hanging branches; my body would have some bruise appendages to add to my barbed wire laceration collection. And to make this adventure, this full freaking fearful adventure, more real, the wind continually howled and moaned through the darkness. If something, or someone were behind me, I would never know it. Glancing at my watch again, I counted four minutes left.

Still within sight of the house, I knew time was too short; I had to leave the security of the trees and make a run for the car. Climbing out onto the road I took off swift and strong. Behind me came that bellow. It was near the house, and I knew the thing had spotted me. Why, I yelled at myself, hadn't I told Kim twenty minutes instead of fifteen? Whatever that creature behind me was, it possessed tremendous speed. It gained most of the ground between us in a matter of seconds. I knew I would never make it to the car. I felt tears well in my eyes and I thought of Kim.

The thing was less than an arm's length behind me when my left foot got in the way of my right, I tripped. The ground came up to meet me instantly and I slid along the gravel like a skipping rock; it hurt a lot, and I thought, great, now I can add road-rash to my collection of injuries for the coroner to note.

I had barely quit sliding before the thing was straddling me, laughing hysterically. One thought came to mind as I stared up into those horrible yellow eyes; congratulations Will Walker, you re freaking dead. Then its powerful hand crashed against my head and all my problems ended.

I had no idea how long I was out, but I wasn't dead. The thing had me draped over its shoulder heading for the woods behind the house. It would be a wise thing, I thought, at least for now, to remain unconscious. So, as Kim sometimes does, I faked it.

Following a short walk into the Pines the thing stopped and lowered me to the ground. Here it comes, I thought, it had taken me into the Pines, probably the very spot where it had killed Deputy Micheles; and now it was going to play with me like a Cat does a mouse, and once it grew tired, rip me apart while I died screaming.

That didn't happen though. Through one open eye, I watched as it bent to open an expertly camouflaged trap door in the ground. Then picking me back up, it threw my fake-unconscious, sore, frightened body back over its shoulder again, and stepped onto a narrow ladder. When it paused to close the hatch above us, I had to fight with myself to keep from panicking. It descended eighteen steps before stepping off the ladder and onto a plank walkway. It then carried me through candle-lit tunnels until we reached our apparent destination; a small dug out room with a thick wooden door. We entered in and I was lowered to the ground. He turned, walked out, closed the big door behind him and locked it. I was left alone.

I waited long enough for it to have gone. Rising to my feet, I grabbed a half burned candle from a holder on the wall beside me. Moving quickly to the thick door I studied it for a way out. There was none, it was solid as a rock. Accepting the fact, I was helplessly trapped, I sat down against the hard dirt wall to try and reason things out. I shivered as the dampness of the tunnel room settled in my bones.

According to my watch, Kim was well on her way to town; that made me feel a little better, but given my circumstance, not a whole lot better. I wondered if Captain Plucousky had received my message yet, and wondered too what Sheriff Davidson s plan of action would be. Everything was happening so fast. I rested my head on my knees and closed my eyes. The pain from my cuts and bruises were now beginning to catch up with me and I ached from head to toe.

I wasn't sure how long I rested like that, but the noise of someone unlocking the door startled me. I considered lying back down and pretending to still be unconscious, but felt it wouldn't matter, if they wanted me awake or dead, they could do either at their leisure; so, I remained sitting and watching what was to come.

Nervously I listened as the lock was unfastened, and the door pushed open. I could not tell who it was, but someone stood in the doorway with a flashlight shining on me. Then they spoke, "Get up and let's go." Climbing to my feet I frowned, recognizing the voice, it was friendly Mr. Wright.

I placed the candle back in its holder. He made a wave with the light's beam indicating I was to step out into the tunnel. "Let's go." When I moved past, I felt the barrel of a revolver poke against my back. "Try anything and it's over. You got it"? I mumbled a yes, and he added, "Good, now get going." I moved through the door and started down the dirty tunnel thinking; whenever Kim's hand gives me a push to get going, it felt soft and warm. But the barrel of a gun pushing me, felt horrible and cold, but then again, not nearly as bad as the bullet that could at any moment, come flying out of its barrel.

Trying to get a conversation going, I told Mr. Wright, "You know, when you talk, you sound just like Clint Eastwood." He hit me in the head with the butt of his revolver and told me to shut up. I wanted to tell him to not do that again if he knew what was good for him, but, like most of us, I clearly understand that lead is not healthy.

We made three lefts and two rights, then ordered to stop. We stood in front of a large sliding metal door.

"Open it and go on in". He told me.

I slid it back and instantly bright light blinded me. It took a few moments for my eyes to adjust, then I entered. My mouth fell open at what I saw. The room was filled with presses, rollers, stacks of bundled paper, and diverse types of machinery. If my guess were correct, all the paper stacked in bundles would be unmarked. The odors of glue and paste filled my nostrils, and hanging on the wall to my left were portraits of Andrew Jackson and Alexander Hamilton. How appropriate I thought. It was then another familiar voice interrupted my thoughts.

"Well Will, what do you think of our little factory?" I turned feeling sick to my stomach and weak in the knees; but I managed to speak. "Quite an operation, Sheriff Davidson." He threw back his head and roared with laughter; but I wanted to cry, feeling incredibly helpless. I found myself thinking about Kim and praying she was able to get help.

Davidson allowed me little time for thought before speaking again.

"Will, my boy. Its s too bad you won't get to see us in action, but at the moment were tearing things down in preparation for our move. And I want you to know it's all because of you and that Black girl of yours".

"It's Afro-American girl of mine." I told him, happy to correct him.

A feeling of accomplishment rushed through me before another surprise came; Davidson's fist caught me off guard landing hard and squarely in the old sollar-plexes. The wind rocketed from my lungs, and I buckled to my knees, gasping for breath.

Get him up. Davidson yelled. Wright pulled me to my feet and held my arms while the compassionate Sheriff backhanded me. Blood filled my mouth; I could taste it. I figured by now, with all my collective wounds, I was beginning to resemble the monster himself, that had carried me down into this underground hell. Davidson yelled again. "Bring her in".

I watched as Kim walked through the sliding door followed by the thing, creature, or whatever it was. Once at my side, she wrapped her arms around me and squeezed with a combination of sympathy and fear. She started to cry. I laid my aching head gently on top of hers enjoying the soft fragrance of her hair. Davidson interrupted again.

"Okay, that's enough lovebirds. I want the two of you to see something." With a gesture of his hand, he singled out the thing. It screamed out a bellow so loud it echoed through the room. Kim and I then watched unbelievably as it began to disrobe. The white-robe garment had no longer hit the floor when it reached up and pulled a vinyl mask from its face, then removed false hair covered gloves from its hands. And lastly, it pulled a disfigured mouthpiece from its mouth. The scary, frightful monster that had killed both Micheles and Johnston now lay in a pile on the floor. Before us stood an exceptionally large, but very huge, normal Afro-American male, who instead of bellowing, now grinned quietly. I didn't know about Kim, but Will Walker felt like a dumb, gullible, unsuspecting ass.

The joke soon over, Davidson ordered the one-time monster, whom he called Rio, back to work. He then turned our way and started leering at Kim. I could feel my heart pound with anger. His hand reached out and ran down the side of her face; she jerked it away and I went crazy. I hit Davidson as hard as I could square under the chin. He staggered back several steps but recovered quickly. I had no idea how bad I hurt him, but his teeth had rattled, and blood flew out of his mouth. Pain or not, he was not happy or impressed by my Rocky impression.

Wiping his mouth with the sleeve of his shirt he told me. "That will cost you greatly, Walker. Turning his head, he yelled at the top of his lungs. Rio, get your big black ass over here. Instantly I was thinking how lucky he was Kim's Mammaw wasn't there. When the big man returned, Davidson ordered him to hold me and for Wright to hold Kim.

With one last look at me, Davidson stepped in front of Kim and stared into her face, with a grin. She stared right back, head held high. Then he tore open her blouse and ripped away the bra. Naked from the waste up, her eyes remained locked on his. Davidson stared at her bare chest and grinned wider. Kim grinned back, "Like what you see, Sheriff? I suggest you do not like them to long; at your age you will strain your eyes and stain your pants."

He lifted his eyes to hers. "You know, you truly are a bitch, but I have to say, you've got two very fine puppies here." Reaching out Davidson gripped them, fondling roughly. I went crazy. I kicked, wiggled, and cursed trying to get loose from Rio's grip. I found myself screaming, "I will kill you Davidson." But he just grinned again and continued fondling Kim.

Realizing my attempts at freeing myself were futile, I stopped struggling. Davidson noted the calm and looked at me. I repeated myself. This time in a cool, calm, self-assured tone. "You're dead, you're dead, dead, dead".

I'm not sure if I scared him or his hands got tired, but he stopped. Stepping back, he ordered Rio and Wright, "Return them to the hole".

Those words were music to my ears. I couldn't wait to get there. Even when the door closed and we heard the lock being snapped into place, I all but cheered. Quickly I took Kim into my arms and squeezed tight. Are you okay?

She nodded, forcing a smile. "I'm fine Will. He didn't hurt you, did he"?

All the buttons of her blouse were missing so she gathered the ends and began tying them into a knot. "Trust me Will", she said as she tied, I'm fine, you've prepared me well for that kind of man-fondling".

I grinned, then moved to the door and checked once again for a sign of potential escape; just as before, the heavy door appeared impregnable.

I returned to Kim's side and we sat against the dirt wall, thinking.

After a short while Kim asked. "Will"?

"Yeah.".

 "Do you think they're going to kill us"?

I put an arm around her and squeezed gently. "Shh, stop worrying. We will get out of this okay. Captain Plucousky will be here soon; and even if he is not, they'll more than likely keep us around in case they need a hostage". It was hard admitting but I knew better. If Plucousky didn t get here and find this underground hiding place before they had everything moved, we were good as dead. I stood up and reached for the candle to examine the door once more. It was still just as strong and me just as discouraged. Kim joined me.

"Can we dig our way out, Will"?

"I don t know, but we may as well try." I returned to the wall where the candle sat. I ripped the small medal holder free, then returned to the door and examined the framework. It consisted of four, four by six timbers, all of which were held in place by long, narrow spikes driven deep into the wall and patterned approximately three feet apart. We decided to try and dig a body size hole between the last two spikes on the lower right-hand side.

Using the candle holder, I began chipping away at the hard, crusted surface. Each stroke met with resistance making it a slow and tedious process. Every few jabs I would stop and listen, knowing that the sound was carrying down the tunnel. I soon began to sweat; it ran down me like a river, with its salty content seeping into every open cut on my body. Adding pain to the collection.

Slowly the outer hard-shell of the wall gave way, permitting access to soft, damp dirt. I smiled with hope. Frantically, I slashed away, slowing down from time to time so Kim could brush away the piling dirt. Within the hour we had the hole just big enough for us to wiggle through. We made a heck of a team.

I wiggled like a worm through the hole and onto the plank walkway on the other side. Kim immediately followed and I pulled her to her feet. There we stood, gloating; but it was short lived. Now, came the hard part, finding our way out without getting caught.

We decided to travel to the right since left lead in the direction of the machine room. At first the candles protruding from the walls seemed to be of little value in lighting the passageways. However, after a time our eyes began focusing quite well; despite our nerves being shot. We were forced to walk slowly so as not to click our heels against the planking and alert anyone to our presence. And yet we both knew that time was about to run out. With the turn of each corner, I expected Rio to jump out with that horrifying bellow of his and cut our throats like he had done to Johnston.

The tunnel turned and twisted like the hollowed body of a cold, dead snake. Panic was no more than a word away, and tears for that matter. We kept asking ourselves, where is that exit? We knew if we didn't t find it soon, our chances of getting out alive would be next to impossible. I wiped my brow with the back of my hand then started praying. That is exactly what I was doing when we rounded the next corner and saw it; the hazy outline of that pretty-little ladder running up the wall to safety. I gave Kim a quick hug and threw Heaven a big kiss.

We were not even to the base of it before we heard footsteps heading in our direction. Quickly we filled the gap and hurryingly scrambled up and out. After closing the lid, we ran for Wright's truck hoping the keys were still in it; of course, they weren't! I knew I had just prayed but I said a bad word anyway; you know the one, it begins with F and ends in K; and it isn't Fire truck. Grabbing Kim's hand I told her with excitement, "Come on, we must get to Johnston's car. It is our only hope.

There would be no second chance, we just had to make it. With most of the distance covered and practically out of breath, we heard the motor to Weight's truck start up; I have no idea where it came from, but we suddenly got a second wind.

By the time we reached the car the headlights from the truck were bearing down on us. I looked in at the ignition. The keys were there, just where Johnston had left them for us. Sliding in, I fired up the engine and squealed away, throwing dirt and grass into the air.

Wright turned off Slayer Road and pulled in behind us. If my guess was correct our patrol car would outrun the pickup. Glancing in my rearview mirror I judged Wright as being no more than six car lengths behind. My speedometer was pressing ninety when we heard the bark of a revolver. They were shooting at us. The bullets didn't hit anywhere, so they were trying to blow out our tires.

I pushed harder on the accelerator and watched in glances as the needle moved to a hundred and five. Simultaneously I heard another shot; this one came crashing through the rear window, buzzed past my ear and went shattering back out again through the front windshield. I ordered Kim down on the seat; under normal circumstances she'd have said, "Yeah right", but this time there was no argument.

As we squealed around winding corners, both vehicles hugged the road in and amazing display of precision. I looked into the mirror again and was blinded by the bright light of the truck's headlights. He had to have a big V-8 in that thing; so, I nixed the possibility of out running him; maybe he'd run out of gas first.

Another bullet came plunging through the rear window again. This time it entered at the lower left-hand corner and came to a damaging halt as it tore into the corner post sitting to my left. The thing ripped a hole in the metal the size of a half dollar. If I'd have moved even a fraction of an inch that post would have been the back of my head.

Then came another shot, this one shattering the rear window completely. Now it would be easy for whoever was doing the shooting to get a clear and accurate aim. I began weaving the car as much as possible without establishing a pattern or risk a roll over. Another shot was fired, and I figured that as being my cue to start praying; it worked for me last time and I sure hoped it worked now. I was halfway through a Hail Mary when I spotted the distant headlights of oncoming cars. "Good Lord, I said aloud, please let that be Plucousky.

I wasn't taking any chances; I had Kim turn the light bar on top of the car, off and on repeatedly, as well as bounce from siren to wail non-stop. We were about to pass the oncoming caravan when I saw the reward of my prayers. Four bright red beacon rays flashed on simultaneously, followed by a symphony of sirens; the prettiest things I ever saw in my life, well, that and a couple of adorable puppies.

Once we passed, I watched through the side view mirror as two of the trailing cars made U turns and began following us; their lights flashing and sirens wailing. With a great big smile, I shouted Thank You Lord, and apologized to Him for saying the F word earlier, than I turned in my seat and gave the fine folks in the pickup truck the middle finger. You don't think the good Lord saw that as hypocritical, do you?

Little by little I decreased my speed and Wright didn't appreciate it, finally he turned off on another road to try and out run the good guys. One car followed him, the other after us. I began breaking and eventually pulled to a stop letting out one long and rejoice full sigh. Kim sat up again and I gave her a big grizzly bear hug. The patrol car pulled in behind us, so we got out of the car and met the two officers halfway.

"Are you two Will and Kim"?

"Yes sir, we are, I'm happy and able to say". The officers looked at the car and back to us. "Looks as though you two had quite an adventure!". This time we all looked at the car. "Oh yeah", I said, "It'd make a great Disneyworld Ride".

The officer went on to explain that Captain Plucousky had been in the lead car and had gone on to the house; that they were to take us there immediately. So, we all piled into their vehicle. On the way I explained about the hidden place underground, the counterfeiting, and Davidson's involvement. I was sorry I did; because the more I told the faster the car went. Driving fast and furious must be a prerequisite to being a police officer. Thankfully, in only a few minutes we were pulling onto Slayer Road though, and when we came to a stop in the front yard, Plucousky was there to meet us.

"Are you two, okay?" When I nodded yes, he asked. "What happened here tonight? I just found the body of another deputy sheriff."

I didn't take time to explain. Instead, I grabbed Kim by the hand and ran for the back of the house, shouting over my shoulder for them to follow. I searched for the trap door and finally found it. I opened it then gave Plucousky a brief rundown. He ordered one of the men to stay on the surface with Kim, then he, two uniformed officers and I descended the ladder.

After what seemed an endless wandering, we stumbled upon the sliding door. Plucousky placed me up against the wall where I watched as he ordered an officer on each side of the door. As soon as they were in place, he took up a position to the right then slid it forcefully open, shouting.

Police Officers, you're under arrest.

All was silent. There was a time lapse of three or four seconds before we heard a gun go off somewhere in the room. Silence once again took over as the loud bark of the weapon faded away. One of the officers looked quickly around the corner spotting a body lying on the floor. It was apparent the person, whoever they were, had shot themselves.

I hoped it wasn't Davison, he deserved worse. With extreme caution, the three men entered the room while I remained at the wall on Plucousky's orders. They were no more than ten feet inside when hell came out of its hole; gunfire and shouting broke out. An endless volley of shots were fired before the room fell calm again. I looked in and saw one of the police officers lying spread eagle on his back.

The remaining officer was rushing to his side and Plucousky was leaning over the body of a man wearing a sheriff s uniform. Leaving the wall, I ran to Plucousky's side. It was Davidson all right. I looked at his blood-soaked body only for a second. Unlike the make-believe violence on Television or at the movies, this was all too real. As much as I disliked Davidson for what he had done, I felt sadness.

Davison had faked taking his own life only to lure Plucousky and the others into the room, knowing a full shoot out would have been a worthless endeavor without an advantage. A pretty good idea I had to admit but thank heaven it turned out the way it did; or at least part of it turned out the way it did.

My mind snapped back to reality, and I looked over at the wounded officer. His unharmed comrade was still at his side. I ran to him and asked it there was anything I could do.

"Yes", he told me. "Stay with him while I go to the surface for help. Our radios won't reach out from down here". I had no more than kneeled when he took off running. Helplessly, I looked down at the officer.

"Don t worry", I told him with as much encouragement as I could muster, "the ambulance will be here soon". I didn't know if he heard me or not, he showed no signs if he did. Captain Plucousky kneeled beside me.

"How is he doing, Will?"

I didn't have time to answer before he started talking to the wounded officer. "How are you doing son?" He asked. The wounded man did not answer. Plucousky began unbuttoning his shirt and looked at the wound. Blood had been steadily soaking into it like a sponge. After he had delicately maneuvered the last button, he took hold of the two sides of the shirt and gently laid them out and away from the office' s chest. A steady surge of blood ran out of a small hole, racing down his abdomen to the beltline. Captain Plucousky pulled out his handkerchief and pressed it firmly over the seeping hole. Even I knew if an ambulance didn't get to him soon, he'd have no chance at all. I looked at Plucousky and asked in a whisper, "Why wasn't he wearing a vest?"

Plucousky just shook his head. He placed a hand on my shoulder. "Will why don t you go to the surface and check on that ambulance. And stay with Kim, I'm sure she'd appreciate your company about now".

I gave him a silent nod and left the room. After a five-minute journey I found the ladder and climbed out. I located Kim leaned against one of the cars wearing a raincoat twice her size. Her hair hung down in long, droopy strands and her face was covered with dirt. She was staring blankly at the ground like a little, lost child. When I stepped in front of her, she looked up and I took her into my arms; it felt good holding her tight; not saying a word she squeezed back, like she never wanted to let go.

Off in the distance we heard more sirens, and I hoped greatly that one of them was the ambulance. Thank God it was. The officer that had come up to call flagged them down and led two paramedics to the tunnel entrance.

After what seemed an eternity one of the paramedics came up out of the hole and returned to the ambulance. He retrieved two black body bags and I felt tears fill my eyes; feeling the officer down there did not deserve to die, and for sure I felt no remorse for Davidson.

When they had the bodies hauled up and placed in the back of the ambulance, Plucousky called it a night for Kim and me. "All right you two", he said, "let's get you home". Without argument we climbed into his car and headed out. Somewhere between Slayer Road and town I drifted off. The stop at Kim's house woke me. I kissed her goodnight and we waited until she was safely inside.

Then we drove to my place. Climbing out I listened drowsily as Captain Plucousky told me to have Kim and myself at his office by 2:00 pm tomorrow. I promised and waved goodnight. Inside I made it as far as the couch and plopped. I yawned, stretched, and yawned again, then closed my eyes. Curling into a ball I sighed. Sleep came then; and wrapped its soft, warm arms around me.

After breakfast I called my doctor's office and explained my sorrowful condition. They made a slot for me, so I let Kim drive me in. Doc looked me over, made a few noises, poked here and their then stuck me with a tetanus shot. Just before leaving the exam room, he ordered me to keep the wounds dry and to take Kim out to dinner and a movie. I told him if I were to do that, I couldn't afford to pay my bill. He studied on it a minute, then recommended we go Dutch treat.

We walked into Plucousky's office at exactly 1:58. He looked up from his desk and told us to have a seat. "So how are you two feeling this morning?" He asked.

I told him fine and Kim told him she was nervous. Flashing a friendly smile, he told her to relax. "The reason I've asked you two here", he said reinforcing his smile, "is to simply make out a statement, no big deal; only routine". He handed us each a form and explained what he wanted. It took approximately twenty minutes and when finished, I asked, "Captain Plucousky, there are a few things bothering me, and I'd like to get them straight".

Plucousky leaned back in his chair. "Sure. Go ahead"

"First, who was that woman in the basement that night? And the other day at the library, Lyle Garson booted me out when I asked questions about the old farmhouse. Is there some connection between Garson and Davidson? And what was the deal with Rio and that ghoulish outfit"?

Captain Plucousky made a thoughtful face. "Okay, Will. Let's see if we can clear your mind. To begin with, the woman in the basement turned out to be Garson's granddaughter. According to the statement Rio gave us, she found an old diary that had been kept by J.W. Peters wife. In it is mention of him spending many nights away from home. Suspecting another woman, she hired a private investigator and had him followed. The investigator's report stated he had been going to the same farmhouse each and every night. Then, according to the diary, the investigator mysteriously came up missing. When that happened, Mrs. Peters herself followed him there, determined to get to the bottom of it. The last entry in the diary spoke of an illegal business that her husband was involved in. That's where the diary ended.

"Wow. What happened to her?"

"Well, we had the Peters history traced and found that Mrs. Peters lived to the age of seventy-six. The diary entries ended when she was around the age of fifty. That stumped us. Everything from here on is strictly police theory. The slayings that night of the legend was real. Peters had witnessed the whole thing all right, but not from behind bushes. We believe Peters was in on it. That he had the rats brought in and kept them on supply. He created the legend in hopes of scaring away the people. Following the murder of the slaves and farm family that night, the tunnels were, up until your involvement, used successfully for counterfeiting; the business we believe made Peters his big money".

"What about the Sheriff?"

"Davidson was part of the rank and file, but there are others higher up. We've a lot more investigation to do."

"And the rats. Why did they suddenly show up again?"

"Somehow Davidson found out about the diary and found it necessary to get rid of anyone who knew about it; just to be safe. We think he brought in the rats because it's a good way to dispose of a body and not leave behind evidence; at least evidence not easy to finish cleaning up. Also, he figured bringing back the rats would keep anyone from being interested in looking into buying the property. Rio was brought in just in case they needed a diversion. If they had to draw attention away, he could simply start killing elsewhere. A monster draws a lot of attention. As for Wright, it turns out he had a previous record and spent sixteen years in prison for counterfeiting, specializing in making money-plates".

"Does Lyle know it was his granddaughter down there?"

Plucousky sighed. "Maybe, but the day you talked to him at the library, that was the last day he was seen anywhere".

Captain Plucousky crossed his legs and pulled out a pack of cigarettes. "Mind"?

We shook our heads, and he lit up, continuing with the story. "Rio assured us he had nothing to do with Lyle Garson's disappearance, and a lie detector test verified it. So, hence forth and furthermore, we have an APB out looking for Garson as we speak, or at least looking for his body. He will turn up eventually".

Plucousky took one more draw on his cigarette and crushed it out in his ashtray. Looking up at us he grinned, "Trying to quit." He leaned back in his chair again, "So now you two know pretty much everything we do, any other questions"?

I thought a minute and couldn't think of any. Kim and I slid our chairs back and stood. I stuck out my hand and Plucousky took it. I gave him a significant squeeze. "Captain," I told him, "We can't thank you enough."

"No," he said," it is us who owe you two the thanks."

Kim and I left his office thankful it was all over. On the way to the car, I slipped my arm around her and asked if there was anything special, she wanted to do. She slipped her hand into the back pocket of my jeans and squeezed my left buttock ever so gently. I raised my eyebrows at her, "Nervis?" I asked her.

"No." she said. "But what do you think about going to my place and I let you play with a couple of cute puppies?"

I grinned. "Okay, if you promise you will not tell your Mammaw."

"Never." She smiled.

Who was I to argue. Of course, I didn't see the crossed fingers hidden behind her back!

END

A. Alex Come'